For my lovely mum, who loved order,
but was always ready to embrace life's surprises,
and to Jo and Dad, with love and thanks

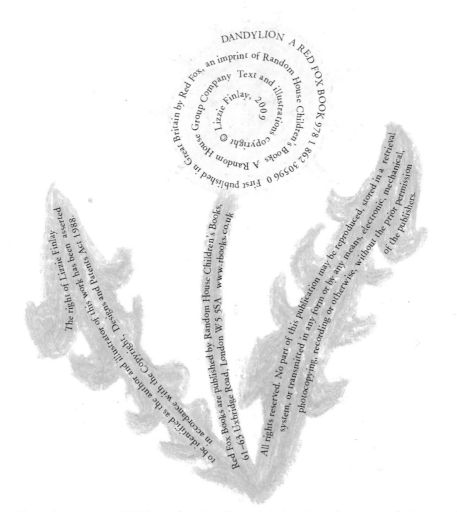

DANDYLION A RED FOX BOOK 978 1 862 30596 0 First published in Great Britain by Red Fox, an imprint of Random House Children's Books A Random House Group Company Text and illustrations copyright © Lizzie Finlay, 2009

The right of Lizzie Finlay to be identified as the author and illustrator of this work has been asserted in accordance with the Copyright, Designs and Patents Act 1988.

Red Fox Books are published by Random House Children's Books, 61–63 Uxbridge Road, London W5 5SA www.rbooks.co.uk

Addresses for companies within The Random House Group Limited can be found at: www.randomhouse.co.uk/offices.htm
THE RANDOM HOUSE GROUP Limited Reg. No. 954009 A CIP catalogue record for this book is available from the British Library.
1 2 3 4 5 6 7 8 9 10 Printed in Singapore.

Dandylion

by Lizzie Finlay

RED FOX

On an otherwise ordinary Tuesday,
Miss Gardener announced,
"Today we have a new boy in our class.
Allow me to introduce . . .
Dandylion to you."

Up sprang the new boy.
He looked **wonderfully unusual**
and **delightfully different**,
bright yellow and
rather scruffy

. . . but they
were too polite
to say so.

Everyone wanted to be Dandylion's new friend.
"Please can he sit next to me?" a little boy asked.
"Thank you," said Miss Gardener.

"Dandylion, this is Basil.
He'll look after you."

On Basil's table they were neatly
painting their flower pictures.

Before long, **Dandylion** was enjoying himself so much that

he
clumsily
spilled
the
paint
water

EVERYWHERE

He was very upset.
The table went quiet.

Then Rosie laughed,
and they all got
the **giggles**.

At lunchtime, Dandylion sat with his new friends.

"Oh, cheese AGAIN,"
moaned Rosie.

"My mum knows I
DON'T like tunafish,"
grumbled Tulip.

"BoRING," huffed
Minty, unwrapping his
usual egg mayo.

But Dandylion's sandwiches
amazed everyone.

"My own *special recipe*," he beamed.

"Chocolate spread,
jelly worms and
candyfloss."

Then it was playtime.
"Let's play tag!" yelled Basil. "Dandylion, you're IT."

"Wait! I know a better game," said Dandylion
with a twinkle in his eyes. "It's called SCARECHASE.

RAAARR
GRRRR
GH!"

he roared
and chased them
all around the playground.

He was surprised when Miss Gardener said,
"Please play nicely like the other children."
"But SCARECHASE is meant to be fun," he thought.

With Dandylion in the class, days skipped by faster

and unexpected things happened.

Like the time Dandylion
brought his pet mouse
Roger to class.

Or when he learned
NOT to wear
costumes to school.

Often Miss Gardener had to stop what she was doing
to have quiet words, making everything late.

One terrible Wednesday, Dandylion's latest adventure landed the children in BIG trouble. Queuing for felt-tip moustaches had made them late for class, and they quickly discovered that it was incredibly naughty to draw on other people's faces.

Miss Gardener was so disappointed,
she could hardly look at them.

At lunchtime, Basil was chosen to be spokesperson.

"We like you, Dandylion . . ." he squirmed.
"It's just that you're not like us . . .
You make life too crazy,
too messy and we get into
too much trouble."

And then, in a small voice, he said,

"I think it might be because you're . . . like . . . a weed."

That day Dandylion went home from school
without bouncing or skipping.
He felt very blue,
although nobody would ever know
because he was always
SO bright yellow.

He didn't go to school
on Thursday.

He thought about things

and decided to try being
less bouncy and to
smarten himself up.

But he didn't like his new, neat look.
His little mind was made up – he was not going back.

"What's happening, my little Dandy?" asked Grandpa.
"You look all serious, with a bow in your hair?"

Wise old Grandpa-Clock always knew what to do,
so Dandylion told him everything.

Grandpa-Clock gave Dandylion a cuddle.

"We all need special people to come and stir up our lives for us," he said. "There'd never be any surprises if everything was always tidy, and we all need surprises."

"They said I'm like a weed," Dandylion sniffed.

"Remember, a 'weed' is only a name given
to a wildflower growing in the wrong place," said Grandpa.
"You're a beautiful wildflower and you can go back and stand tall."

Without Dandylion, apple-pie order had returned to Miss Gardener's classroom. But the children missed his **bright sunny yellow** face. They missed the **bouncing** and the **excitement** and even the **spills** and the **mess**

"We miss Dandylion," Basil announced after lunch. The whole class nodded.

"Hmmmm, I've got an idea . . ." Miss Gardener said.

Parents/Guardians

That day everyone went home with a school letter and a smile on their face.

On Friday, everything was different
in Miss Gardener's classroom.
There were bright colours everywhere.
The children were busily making things.

Out of the blue, Dandylion bounced in –
just in time for extraordinary sandwiches.

Everyone **cheered** when they saw him.
"Hello, Dandylion," Miss Gardener beamed.
"Today is Wildflower Day."
The whole class was wearing
sunny yellow.

Dandylion now felt like a wildflower in the right place.